recycling & reusing

Rubber

Ruth Thomson

Photography by Neil Thomson

A+

Smart Apple Media

First published in 2006 by Franklin Watts
338 Euston Road, London NW1 3BH

Franklin Watts Australia, Hachette Children's Books
Level 17/207 Kent Street, Sydney NSW 2000

Editor: Rachel Cooke, Design: Holly Mann, Art Director: Rachel Hamdi

Additional photography
Franklin Watts 4/5, 6tl, 6tr, 6bl, 7tr, 9tr, 9cl, 9bl, 9br, 21tr; JCB 7tl; Continental 8tr, 8bl;
Ecoscene/Christine Osborne 9l; Environment Agency UK 11bl; Earthship Inc. 12, 13; Agripicture
Images 24; Playtop 27.

Published in the United States by Smart Apple Media
2140 Howard Drive West, North Mankato, Minnesota 56003

Library of Congress Cataloging-in-Publication Data

Thomson, Ruth, 1949–
Rubber / by Ruth Thomson.
p. cm. — (Recycling and reusing)
Includes index.
ISBN-13: 978-1-58340-941-1
1. Rubber—Juvenile literature. I. Title.

TS1890.T65 2006
678'.29—dc22   2006000171

9 8 7 6 5 4 3 2 1

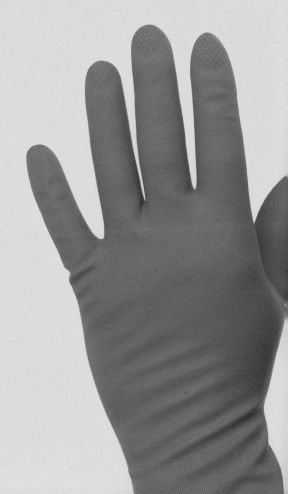

Contents

What is rubber like?

Rubber is an unusual **material** that bends, stretches, and bounces.

Rubber is elastic.
When you pull a rubber band, it stretches. When you let go, it springs back into shape.

Rubber is springy.
If you drop a rubber ball, it bounces back up again.

Rubber is airtight.
When you blow up a rubber balloon, it holds air inside.

6

Rubber has a soft surface that grips well.
Rubber tires do not slip on soft, muddy ground.

Rubber is waterproof.
When water falls on rubber, it is not absorbed. Rubber boots keep your feet dry on wet ground.

LOOK AND SEE

- Fill a balloon with water. Does any water leak out?
- Put a magnet over a balloon. Does anything happen?

- Stretch a balloon as far as you can. What happens when you let go?

Boing! Boing!
Sports such as tennis and basketball are played with rubber balls.

Making rubber

Natural rubber is made from **latex**. This is the sticky white **sap** found under the bark of the tall rubber tree.

Rubber trees

Rubber trees are grown in **plantations** in warm, wet countries near the **equator**. Most plantations are in Malaysia, Indonesia, and Thailand.

Rubber trees grow in rows.

Collecting the latex

Plantation workers, called **tappers**, cut a slanting slit in the tree bark and attach a spout and a small cup underneath. The latex runs down the groove into the cup. The latex has tiny bits of rubber in it.

The tappers tap each tree every few days.

Separating the rubber

Workers tip the latex into a tank and add **acid**. This makes the rubber bits clump together into solid lumps.

Rolling the rubber

The rubber clumps pass through rollers, which squeeze out all the water and roll the clumps into flat sheets. These are hung on racks to dry.

Sheets of rubber drying

The rubber is sent to **factories** all over the world, where it is shaped into all sorts of things.

IT'S A FACT

Not all rubber is natural. Most rubber is now made in factories with chemicals made from **oil**. This is called **synthetic** rubber.

LOOK AND SEE

Look around your home to see how many everyday things are made with rubber.

Rubber-covered electric cable

Kitchen spatula

Floor mat

Jar seals

- *What do the objects feel like?*
- *Why are they made of rubber?*

Flashlight

Kitchen gloves (made of latex)

Tons of tires

Cars and trucks have rubber tires with a pattern of grooves and ridges called the tread. The tread helps tires grip the road, even when it is wet. When the tread becomes smooth, tires are worn out.

Throwing away tires

It is not easy to get rid of old tires. Rubber does not **rot** if it is buried. Burning rubber can produce harmful **gases** and thick smoke. Piling tires in a dump is a fire risk and offers shelter for **pests** such as rats. The tires hold water and can be a breeding ground for mosquitoes.

Reusing old tires

Old tires are so strong, heavy, and springy that they can be **reused** in all sorts of places.

Tires often hang along harbor walls and over the sides of ships. They protect both the ships and the walls from damage.

Bulky barriers

Go-kart circuits and bike tracks are often lined with safety barriers made of tires.

Embankments and walls

Tire **bales** make good **embankments** against floods. Each one is made from 100 used tires squashed and tied together.

Walls made of used tires tied together with rope or wire can help prevent soil **erosion** on soft, crumbly hillsides.

Heavy weights

Farmers use tires as weights to hold down plastic sheeting over their cut grass. The grass turns into **silage** that cows will feed on in the winter.

Extraordinary earthships

Michael Reynolds, an American architect, designs houses that people can build themselves using waste tires and soda pop cans. He calls these houses "earthships."

Each tire is laid in place and packed tightly with earth to make a building block.

Harnessing nature

Earthships use the power of nature. They are heated by the sun and catch water from rain and snow. They make their own electricity from **solar** and wind energy, process their own **sewage**, and have a greenhouse for growing food.

The tires are arranged in staggered lines, just like clay bricks, to make the walls.

Solid walls

The earthships have a row of U-shaped rooms. Each room has three solid tire walls. These are covered with mud and plaster to create a smooth finish. The front wall has glass panels to trap the energy from the sun.

Empty aluminum pop cans make good fillers for walls that do not bear any weight.

The greenhouse hallway gets light all the time. It is a good place to grow plants.

The thick, heavy walls of the rooms behind the hallway store heat by day and slowly release it by night.

The floor is made of smooth **adobe**.

The windows are made of two layers of glass. This helps trap heat.

The wooden beams are made from local trees.

Tire transformations

People have transformed tires into unusual things.

Pretty planters

1. This African man cuts off one side of tires to make planters. Here he is painting the outside of one.

2. He glues plastic mesh across the base of the planter. This lets water drain out when the planter is filled with soil and flowers.

3. He sells the planters by the roadside to passing drivers.

14

Comfortable swings

Tires can be cut to make swings.

The curved shape of the tire makes a perfect seat.

A clever climbing frame

Rows of old tires make rungs for this climbing frame in India.

A tower for trees

A tower of tires protects this young tree from damage but gives it plenty of room to grow.

Rescued rubber

In some places, people cut old tires into pieces and craft the rubber into useful new objects.

Tire treasures

In Morocco, there are workshops that specialize in making buckets and water containers from old tires.

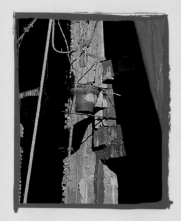

Builders use the buckets for carrying rubble or bricks.

People use the buckets at home for holding wood or tools.

Donkey owners use the buckets for feeding their animals.

Careful cutting

This man is using a very sharp knife to cut and slice tires into thin strips.

Shaping the strips

He cuts the strips into pieces. He glues and nails them together to make objects like these.

Picture frame

Container

Water bottle

Bridles and blinkers

Donkeys sometimes wear bridles and blinkers made of reused scraps of rubber. The rubber is comfortable for them to wear. It is also far cheaper than leather.

Rubber shoes

Shoes often have rubber soles and heels. The springy rubber soaks up the shock of your footsteps on hard ground and makes walking more comfortable.

In countries where shoes are expensive, cobblers make cheap, durable shoes with rubber from old tires.

Rubber sole   Rubber heel

Sturdy sandals

In South Africa, cobblers make sandals entirely from rubber. They use white-walled tires from vans and cut patterns into the rubber.

Soft slippers

In Morocco, there is a long tradition of making soft slippers with leather uppers and soles. Now, some shoemakers make these slippers with tougher scrap rubber soles.

Bath shoes

In Egypt, people wear shoes for bathing before they go to prayers in a mosque. This cobbler makes shoes from wood and scrap rubber, which will not rot when they get wet.

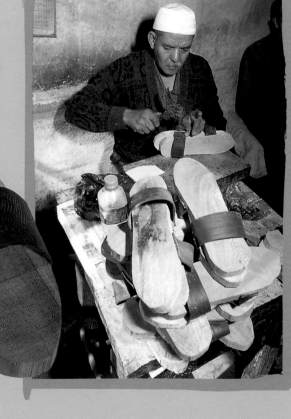

Inner tube inventions

People make unexpected things with discarded rubber **inner tubes**. It is easy to cut these soft tubes with scissors.

Fancy footwork

Children play in the narrow alleys of towns in Morocco. Instead of using a ball, they make a bundle of inner tube strips tied tightly together. They try to keep the bundle up in the air for as long as possible.

Bundle of tied-up rubber strips

Tires for toys

In parts of Africa, craftsmen make toy bikes, trucks, and cars from scrap metal and wire. They wind strips of inner tube around the wheels to make the tires.

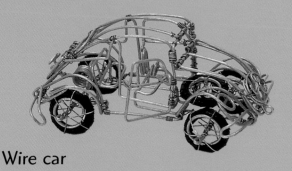

Wire car

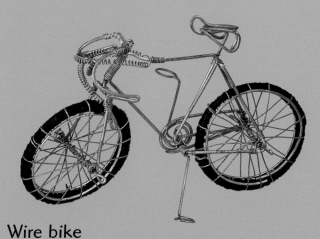

Wire bike

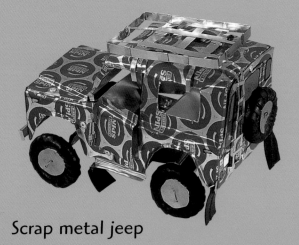

Scrap metal jeep

- *If you have a bicycle, keep the tires well-inflated so that they last longer.*

- *Learn how to fix the inner tube if you get a puncture.*

In countries where inner tubes are expensive, people patch them over and over again.

Remarkable rubber

Inventive designers are reusing inner tubes to make fashion accessories.

Beads and bracelets

In South Africa, craftswomen make bracelets with rubber beads or braided rubber strips.

1. To make beads, they punch circles of rubber out of discarded truck inner tubes.

2. They punch holes in the circles to turn them into beads.

3. They string the beads together on a strip of rubber and finish the bracelet off with a rubber clasp.

Braided rubber bracelets

You're framed

Bands of inner tube, joined with knotted rubber strips and washers, make a sturdy picture frame.

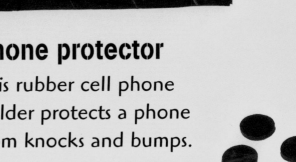

Phone protector

This rubber cell phone holder protects a phone from knocks and bumps.

Numbered bags

In South Africa, when people move to a new town, they have to change their car license plates. A clever car salesman had the idea of joining discarded license plates with a piece of inner tube to make unique handbags like this one.

Rubber remnants

Since rubber is tough and waterproof, it is a perfect material to reuse outside.

A soft surface

Tires are chopped into small pieces and mixed with sand for horse tracks.

The surface is comfortable for horses. It also protects riders from injury if they fall off.

A water trap

In countries with scarce rain and sandy soil, it is hard for plants to grow. Old tires and inner tubes are ideal for making water traps.

Water trap

Side wall of a tire

Circle of inner tube glued to the tire

This water trap has been left uncovered to show how well it holds water. Gaps between water traps let some water drain away so the land does not become too wet.

People dig a trench in the ground and lay water traps in rows. Then they cover the traps with soil and sow seeds.

Plants that grow on top of water traps grow far better than those without this extra water supply.

Recycling rubber

Millions of scrap truck tires are **recycled** into tiny granules called rubber crumb. These can be bonded together to make a new material.

Surprising stationery

Notebook covers and pencil cases made from recycled rubber are very durable.

Notebook

USED TO BE CAR TIRE...

Pencil case

A mouse pad

The rubber surface is smooth enough to use as a mat for a computer mouse.

Mouse pad

Finely shredded

Tires are fed through several grinders with sharp blades. Each one chops the rubber into smaller and smaller pieces.

A safe surface

The recycled rubber bits are glued together into a thick layer. This is laid under new playground surfaces. If children fall, they are less likely to hurt themselves.

Glossary

acid a kind of harsh chemical

adobe a mixture of mud and straw

bale a large bundle

bonded joined together firmly

embankment a steep bank or mound built up to keep water within a certain place

equator the imaginary line around the center of Earth, halfway between the north and south poles

erosion the gradual wearing away of something, such as soil or rock

factory a building where things are made in large numbers using machines

gas a substance that is neither a solid nor a liquid; air is a mixture of gases

inner tube the hollow tube inside a tire, which is filled with air

latex the milky sap of the rubber tree

material a substance used to make something else

natural found in the world; not made by people or machines

oil a sticky, black liquid found under the ground or sea

pest an insect or animal that eats crops or destroys things

plantation a large area of land used for growing only one type of plant, such as rubber or banana trees or coffee plants

recycle use an existing object or material to make something new

reuse use again

rot the natural way a material slowly breaks down into lots of smaller, different substances

sap the liquid that carries food around a plant

sewage the waste from toilets in buildings

silage green fodder for animals that is stored for winter feed

solar powered by energy from the sun

synthetic not natural; made by people

tapper someone who slits the bark of a rubber tree to let the latex flow out

waterproof not letting water in or out

Guess what?

- Nearly 80 percent of the world's natural rubber is grown in just three countries—Malaysia, Indonesia, and Thailand.

- More than two-thirds of all rubber produced is used to make tires for cars, trucks, tractors, and airplanes.

- Most cars use 17 tires in their lifetime.

- Tire dumps often catch fire. These are almost impossible to put out and can burn for weeks. They can poison the soil and nearby water and pollute the air.

- According to the Agricultural Research Service, more than 265 million tires are discarded each year.

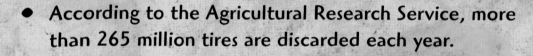

Useful Web sites

http://www.epa.gov/recyclecity/
See how Dumptown became Recycle City with fun games and interesting facts about recycling rubber and other materials

http://www.olliesworld.com/planet/
A fun, interactive Web site that includes information and tips about reusing and recycling

http://www.nike.com/nikebiz/nikego/
Learn about the Nike Reuse-A-Shoe program and how old shoes can be recycled to make basketball courts, running tracks, and more

http://www.planetpals.com/earthday.html
Projects and information about Earth Day, America Recycles Day, and other events that promote recycling

Index

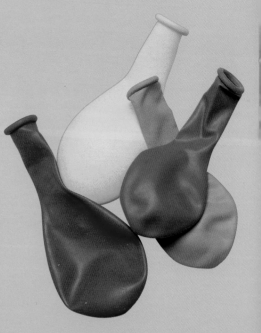